CW00797254

Dead Town

Series 1

The Scripts

Written by

Peter Mckeirnon

ISBN-13: 978-1535278294

ISBN-10: 1535278293

Acknowledgements

Dead Town would not be possible without the following people. Thank you for everything you have done to make this series a reality.

Andy Savage, Graham Kirk, Neil Gallagher, Michael Hagen, Karl Davies, Ian Hewitt, Paul Leech, Andrew Butterworth, Matt McGurty, Josh Poole, James Nemo, Danny Boardman, Andy Coffey, Victoria Kathryn Smith, Steve Sears, Colin Webster, Stuart Davies, David Paul, Jackie Mercer, Nathan Dawber, Lorna Gibson, Jack Cross, everyone at Smart Storage and Lill's Café, Oliver Clay, Kay Mckeirnon, Rod Hay, Ilan Sheady, Adam Choat, Robyn Walker, Iain McCarroll, Sara McCarroll, John Williams, Mike Facherty, Steven Ford, Andy Oakley, Claire M Johnson, Craig Jenkins, Sally Sebok, Jean Mckeirnon, Julia Kelly, Jobie McPartland, Julie Redican, Peter Dreer, Bernie O'Flaherty, Mel baker Owen, Laurence Shone, Drew Ridley, Andy

Osborne, Katie Watson, Dean Garner,
Paul Prescott, Stephen Adams, Sharon
'Mamma Zombie' Greenwood, Chris
Unsworth, Greg Walker, David Wilson,
Phil Brake, Andy Coffey, Rianna Farmer,
Jean Mckeirnon, Belynda Oates, Steve
Howarth, Jonny LeRoy, Wesley Jones.

Episode Guide

Episode 1 'Road to Nowhere'

John eats mayonnaise for a living. At least he did until his boss turned into a zombie then tried to eat him. Now all he wants to do is find his daughter Emily and keep her safe. But in zombie infested Runcorn, even simple tasks like crossing the street or finding batteries for your vintage Sony Walkman have become a matter of life or death.

Armed with a mayonnaise stirring paddle and porno mags for armour; John, along with his retro best friend, 80s Dave and his apocalypse obsessed brother, Butty begin the search for his daughter.

Episodes 2 'This Must Be The Place'

Evening is drawing in and John is no closer to finding his daughter. Seeking

Shelter they take refuge in the home of Brittain, a 17 year old agoraphobic traveller that has never left his house. However, after a motivational speech from 80s Dave, everything changes but will Brittain's new found sense of adventure end in disaster?

Episodes 3 'Once in a Lifetime'

It's early morning and Butty convinces John and 80s Dave that if they are to be successful in finding Emily, then they need to stock up on apocalyptic weaponry. Luckily he knows just the place, a storage lock up where Butty has rented units full of supplies for every end of the world scenario you can think of. Spider badgers, mutated women with laser tits, the French… he's got it covered. But with 80s Dave and John unable to keep quiet it isn't long till the lock up is filled with dead fucks and our quirky survivors are faced with a horde of zombies, hell bent on feasting on human flesh!

Episode 1

'Road to Nowhere'

Scene 1 - Ext - Daytime - Road

A road, overgrown and unkempt. A car has broken down and the bonnet is up.

80s Dave is leaning against the car smoking a cigarette. He is nodding along to music.

John Diant is sitting on the curb with his head in his hands.

The boot of the vehicle is also up, obscuring Butty from view.

                    Dave

What's up with your face? You look like you've just had a rectal examination and the doctor left his finger up their a little too long.

John doesn't respond.

                    Dave

Hey, remember this morning when we were just average no marks working in a mayonnaise factory? Then the boss shat his pants, puked up a kidney and tried to eat us? Funny that wasn't it?

John lifts his head to look at Dave. He is not amused.

Scene 2 - Ext - Daytime - outside the mayonnaise factory.

Flash back

Dave and john are looking at their manager who is lying face down in a puddle of puke.

John

Do you think he's dead?

Dave

Probably kid. You could always go and check for a pulse?

Close up of their managers head, covered in puke and gunk.

John

7

I would rather put shit in my hands and clap than touch his skin.

Dave

Hang on ace, I've had an idea. I'll be right back.

John

Where are you going?

Dave

To the factory. I'll be back in a jiffy.

Dave runs off and John takes out his mobile phone and tries calling for an ambulance but gets no answer. He then calls his daughter but gets her answerphone.

John

Emily, it's your Dad. Please call me when you get this and stay in-doors OK? Do not go outside. Something very strange is happening. Love you.

He puts his phone back in his pocket then looks towards his boss, slowly and tentatively moving towards him.

John

Simon? Are you alright mate?

Dave appears behind john holding a large mayonnaise stirring paddle.

Dave

I'm back!

John

Christ Dave don't creep up on me like that! I've tried calling for an ambulance but I couldn't get through. Emily isn't answering her phone either. What's that for?

Dave

For making mayonnaise.

John

I know that Andrew Ridgeley. I meant why do you have it?

Dave

I thought we could use it to flip him onto his back. Then you can place an

ear to his mouth to see if he's
breathing. Cunt.

John

Don't call him a cunt Dave. He might be
dead, you shouldn't speak ill of the
dead.

Dave

Dead or not he's still a cunt. Worst
fucking manager I've ever had. In fact,
he better not be dead as he still owes
us money for 3 weeks overtime, cunt!
And he's wearing a wig.

John

That's not a wig.

Dave

That, is most definitely a Wig. Tenner
says it's a fucking syrup.

John tentatively leans in to Simon and
reaches to remove the wig from his
head. Just as he is about to touch him,
Simon lifts his head out of the puddle
of puke, groaning and snarling. Dave is

smiling in awe and John looks petrified.

                    John

                (running away)

                  Fuck me!

Scene 3 - Ext - Daytime - Road.

                    John

No Dave it wasn't funny, it was a nightmare! This whole day is turning into a fucking nightmare. What the hell are you listening to anyway, it sounds bloody awful from over here? Like a cat slowly having its claws ripped from its paws.

                    Dave

Public Image Ltd, fucking awesome lar. John Lydon at his best. Pure 80s Gold. Your bro said he has a vintage hi-fi with a double tape deck at his place. I'll pick up a blank cassette tape whilst we're out and do you a copy later.

John

Dave, you do know what year it is don't you? You can't just pop out to the shops for a blank cassette tape. People don't use them anymore.

Dave

Yeah well, people are dicks.

There is a short pause. Dave notices John's distress.

Dave

We'll find your daughter John, we'll get to Emily. So what if the car's knackered. It won't take long to find something else. It's the zombie apocalypse, there will be abandoned cars everywhere.

John

You don't have to stay Dave. Don't you want to check on your family?

Dave

Family? You mean my folks? Fuck them lar. They don't give a shit about me, never have. As soon as I was old enough to wipe my own arse they left me to it. Why should I care what happens to them? They're in Liverpool anyway, I could never get there in time. No mate, we're going to get Emily, she'll be needing her dad and her whacko Uncle.

Butty - Voice from behind the raised car boot

I heard that.

John

I appreciate you sticking around mate, it means a lot. But fuck me Dave, zombies! It's one of those impossible scenarios that would never happen but people talk about how awesome it would be if it did. Well as it turns out zombies, are not awesome.

Dave

(Inspecting his blood stained mayonnaise stirring paddle)

They are a little bit.

John

How much longer Butty, we need to get moving?

                    Butty

        You can't rush perfection!

Scene 4 - Ext - Daytime - Road

We see a zombie shuffling on to the road. We can see John, Dave and the car in the distance.

Scene 5 - Ext - Daytime - Road

Back to John, Dave and the car. Dave notices the slowly approaching zombie.

                    Dave

            Dead fuck alert.

                    John

Oh God not another one, I can't kill anyone else.

                    Dave

Another one, are you shitting me? We've only had a scrap with two and I killed both of the bastards!

Scene 6 - Ext - Daytime - Outside the mayonnaise factory

Flashback

We see the John and Dave's zombie boss on the floor moaning and groaning.

We see Dave looking down on him, about to thrust the mayonnaise stirring paddle downwards.

Dave

(Repeatedly bashing the zombies head with the paddle)

Wig wearing twat! Fucking 3 weeks overtime! You NEVER... FUCKING... PAID... US! Fucking little bell end, fucking wig, fucking twat... DIE!

We see a close up of the final blow decapitating the now mangled head of Simon.

Scene 7 - Ext - Daytime - Road.

John

Yes but don't forget I helped you take down the big guy.

Scene 8 - Ext - Daytime - Outside the mayonnaise factory

A large zombie appears, shuffling and moaning towards John and Dave. Having noticed the zombie, a petrified John taps Dave on the shoulder, pointing at the zombie.

Dave

(Teasing the zombie)

Come 'ed big lad, there's more flavour in me than a Ginsters Pasty! Come and get ya din dins ya massive fuck wod!

The big zombie shuffles towards Dave, his arms reaching out trying to grab him.

John walks towards Simon's decapitated wig wearing head and takes it in his hands. With a face of repulsion he gags before puking heavily. Wiping the puke from his mouth John takes the head and walks up behind the zombie, tapping him on the shoulder.

The big zombie turns and John whacks him across the face with Simon's head, sending the wig flying through the air. The big zombie barely moves. Dave pisses himself laughing.

                    Dave

    I told you it was a fucking wig!

Scene 9 - Ext - Daytime - Road.

                    Dave

    You hit him in the face… with a face!
    Whilst I'm not sure that was exactly
    classed as helping it was fucking funny
                    Ace.

                    John

          I distracted him.

                    Dave

    You did indeed kidda, you did indeed!

Scene 10 - Ext - Daytime - Outside the mayonnaise factory

John looks down at the zombie head in his hands then back up to the big zombie facing him. The big zombie groans and reaches out to John. There is a squelch and the zombie jolts before stopping dead in its tracks. Dave has inserted the paddle into the back of the zombies head

                    Dave

              Fuck me lar!

Scene 11 - Ext - Daytime - Road

Dave is admiring his blood stained mayonnaise stirring paddle.

                    Dave

Not only is it great for stirring a large vat of mayonnaise it's also an awesome zombie twatter! I do love my Battle Paddle.

                    John

Battle Paddle? Is that what you're
calling it now?

Dave

Well I was going to call it John Diant
2 as it's dense and does your head in!

Dave's looks to the incoming zombie
slowly shuffling towards them.

Dave

Come on Butty lad hurry up. We've got a
zombie heading our way and your brother
is going to have a meltdown if we don't
get moving soon. What could you
possibly be doing that's taking so
long?

We here the car boot slam shut and
Butty steps out.

He is wearing large leather boots which
cover his ankles. Protecting the boots,
are several metal plates. On his legs
are the tightest jeans you have ever
seen. Over his knees are skateboarding
pads and, around his waist, a tool belt
which holds several knives of various
sizes, a crowbar, sling shot, a set of

darts and a bag of marbles. Over his stomach and chest is a stab proof vest. Covering his elbows are more skateboarding pads. Protecting his lower arms are shin pads and over his upper arms are porno mags. On his head is a biker's helmet.

                    Butty

                    This!

John and Dave laugh.

                    John

Do you remember when we were kids and we used to make our own costumes and pretend we were Transformers? Well that's what you look like now. Optimus Shite - Halfwit in Disguise! Go on then let's hear it, explain yourself.

                    Butty

There's nothing to explain. What you're looking at here is the perfect zombie protection suit.

                    John

I wouldn't really call it a suit. More of a mixed bag of crap you found lying about the house.

Butty

Crap? You have a lot to learn little brother. You see these boots? Big and heavy and almost impossible to damage. There's not a zombie roaming the Earth that could chomp through these bad boys and just to make sure, I've covered them in metal plates. Not only extra protection but great for causing damage should I have to boot any of the bastards!

Dave

That's a nice selection of porno mag's you've got taped to your arms. What's that all about? Once you've finished bashing zombies does it make you want to bash something else?

Butty

The thing with porno mags Dave, is that they are very well laminated. Easy to wipe clean you see and it also makes them difficult to tear, rip or even bite through. This makes 'grumble' magazines such as Razzle, Bumper Booties, Milk Maids and Filthy GILFS perfect zombie armour!

Dave

And what about those Skinny Jeans? They're so tight they look like they've been painted on. I can even tell what side you get dressed. They can't be comfortable? Your junk looks like a squashed bull frog! It's almost putting me off me smokes!

Butty

Skinny jeans are perfect anti zombie trousers. Nothing for them to grab hold of you see? In fact, I reckon the next chance we get, we pick up skinny jeans for everyone.

Dave

Fuck that lar, I'd rather take my chances than squeeze into those things.

John

Let's move away from your denim leggings for a second and talk about that thing on your head.

Butty

And what of it?

John

You look like a Poundland Judge Dredd!

Dave

Judge Dreadful! No offence kid.

Butty

None taken Dave. How can I be offended by a man that looks like he's stepped out of a Wham! video and walks around carrying a giant spoon?

Dave

Touché Butty lad touché! This isn't a spoon by the way, it's an effective zombie killing weapon.

Butty

Yes I've looked over your 'Battle Paddle' Dave. Clumsy and impractical which was proven this morning when I had to come to your rescue.

Scene 12 Ext - Daytime - Outside the mayonnaise factory

Dave is holding on to the Battle Paddle which is still wedged into the back of the head of the large zombie. The paddle is the only thing keeping the zombie on its feet.

Dave

You should see this Ace, his fucking brain is seeping out! And listen…

Dave wiggles the paddle and squelching is heard as the shovel end moves inside the dead zombie's head. John starts to gag and moves around trying hard not to vomit.

Groaning is heard and 2 zombies are seen to be approaching.

John

Dave come on we've got to move.

Dave tries to free his paddle but it won't budge.

                    John

         Dave, get a move on, we need to go,
                    NOW!

                    Dave

         I'm trying kid but me paddle's stuck,
                 it won't come out!

                    John

         "Leave the paddle in his head, come on
              we don't have any time!

                    Dave

         Leave the paddle? I'd rather jack than
                 Fleetwood Mac!

With herculean effort, Dave pulls the paddle out of the zombies head. We hear a car approaching as the zombie falls to the floor.

A car screeches to a halt and Butty jumps out, running towards the 2 approaching zombies. With 2 clean kills he takes them out, thwarting them both with a crowbar. Once dead, Butty turns from the zombies and walks casually towards John and Dave.

                    Butty

    Good morning little brother. I
  remembered how pathetic you are and
   thought you might need saving. Who's
  the throwback with the oversized spoon?

Scene 13 - Ext - Daytime - Road

                    Dave

    Bollocks! I was fine. Anyway, some
  rescue attempt. We only got 2 minutes
   up the road before your fucking car
               broke down!

Groaning is heard and we see that the
shuffling zombie is closing in.

                    Dave

   Suppose I best take care it. John has
  the gag reflex of a new born and Butty,
   well… Your jeans are so tight if you
    moved with any kind of speed, I'd be
   worried you'd end up split in three!
  Plus we've got to get moving. I've got

26

four tabs left and if you think I'm a sarcastic twat now you should see me without any smokes.

Dave with his Battle Paddle, walks towards the zombie. Behind him, Butty reaches into his utility belt and retrieves a dart.

Like he is stepping up to the oche at Lakeside, about to throw for the world Darts Championship, Butty aims then with an over the top throwing movement, launches the dart towards the zombie, hitting it in the forehead, sending it falling backwards to the ground, dead.

Dave

Shit in my fucking gob!

Butty struts forward and walks between John and Dave, legs slightly apart like he has been in the saddle all day.

Butty

Legs go get Emily bitches!"

Show music starts. Slow motion shot of John, Dave and Butty leading, walking forward (Reservoir Dogs style). Butty is eating a banana, Dave is smoking and John looks like he's going to have a breakdown at any minute.

John - Voice over

"My name is John Diant, Father to a teenage daughter, brother to a survivalist loon and friend to a retro piss taking Scouser. This morning my town went to shit and now the dead are roaming the streets. My daughter is missing and I will do everything I can to find her.

End.

Episode 2

'This Must Be The Place'

Scene 1 - Ext - Early evening - A street with a walled garden.

Butty runs in to shot. A zombie hand reaches up from the wall behind him. Using a sawn off snooker cue, Butty thrashes down, killing the zombie. He signals from John and Dave to join him. They rush over.

John

We should have found Emily by now, she could be anywhere.

Dave

We'll be with her in no time Ace. As Bon Jovi once said, you gotta keep the faith lar. Why have we stopped Butty lad?

Butty

Because it will be dark soon and we need somewhere to stay for the night.

John

What about Emily? We've barely started looking for her and you want us to stop for the night? Anything could have happened to her.

Butty

You're forgetting one thing little brother. Emily is family. She's my niece which means, she has my blood. She's a fighter and is well trained in the ways of apocalyptic survival. What do you think we do when she stays with me of a weekend? Watch Vampire Dairies and braid each other's hair? As long as she's remembered her training she'll be just fine. No doubt she will be doing the same as us.

Butty runs off.

Dave

What the fuck is Vampire diaries?

John

What's the greatest Vampire movie ever made?

Dave

The Lost Boys.

John

Well it's like that, but complete shit.

John walks after Butty and Dave follows.

Scene 2 - Ext - Early evening - Outside the front door of an end of terrace house.

Butty then John and Dave move in front of the house door.

Butty

There doesn't appear to be anyone home. Looks like we're going to have to break in?

Butty and John look at Dave.

Dave

Oh fuck off! Just because I'm a Scouser doesn't mean I know how to break in to a house. Just kidding, of course I do! Move out of the way cock floppers and let the master get to work.

Dave swaggers to the front door. He tried the door handle but it is locked.

John - To Butty

I bet he tries to break it down with his battle paddle.

Dave

No I'm not! Smart arse.

Dave looks fresh out of ideas and doesn't know what to try next. He raises his battle paddle and goes to smash the door when…

Man's voice from behind the door

Don't even think about it. I'm like 7ft and I'm a black belt in dishing out ass whoopin's!

Butty

(Stepping up to the door)

We are not looking for trouble but if you don't open the door right now, I'm going to rip off your head and feed it to your arse! DO YOU UNDERSTAND?"

Dave

Great that Butty lad. Did you never fancy a job with the Samaritans or maybe as a police negotiator? You know, the ones they send into delicate situations to keep the peace? Because you'd be fucking spot on kid.

The front door swings open and a middle aged man dressed like a teenager is stood in the doorway looking nervous.

Brittain

Please don't kill me! I was only joking, I'm not really 7ft and I'm only 17. I don't even own a belt never mind a black one.

Dave - To John

Did he just say he was 17?

John

Maybe he's had a hard life.

                    Dave

Hard life? He must have a good internet
                connection.

                    John

                    Why?

                    Dave

Because anyone that says they're 17
years old but looks like that must be
    wanking for queen and country.

            Butty - To Brittain

Calm down soft lad we're not going to
                hurt you.

Butty barges passed and enters the
house.

John approaches Brittain.

                    John

Sorry about intruding like this but all
    we need is somewhere to stay for the
night. We'll be gone first thing in the
morning, I promise. And forget what my
brother said, nobody is going to kill
                    you.

John enters and Dave approaches Brittain.

Dave

Don't listen to Butty. He wasn't to know you've obviously got some kind of wasting disease.

Dave pushes passed Brittain and enters the house.

Brittain is left in the open doorway looking very concerned. He hesitates, then reaches out and grabs the door to close it without stepping outside.

Scene 3 - Int - Early evening - Brittain's living room.

Butty is sat at the window, occasionally peeping through the closed curtains. Dave is sat on the floor going through Brittain's DVD collection. John is sat on the couch.

John

Does anyone know what time it is? It feels like we've been here for hours.

Butty takes a sly look at the clock which is on a table out of John's view,

then he looks through the curtains
again.

Butty

Judging by the angular vector of the
moon, I'd say it's 6pm and we've been
here for 20 minutes. Don't panic John.
We'll resume our search for Emily at
first light

John

Since when have you been able to use
the moon to tell time?

Dave

He hasn't, there's a clock over there
in plain sight. He's pulling your
plonker kid. Yanking your chain. Quite
witty for a man who dresses like an
extra from The Warriors. Speaking of
awesome 80s movies, there's some
cracking films here boys. He's even got
the Police Academy box-set. Fucking
boss lar. I reckon we go with Police
Academy 1 to 6 only, as 7 was made in
the 90s and is so fucking awful, I'd
rather shit the bed than watch it
again. It will be morning by then and
we can go looking for Emily fuelled on
awesome 80s comedy

John

We're not watching Police Academy, Dave.

Dave

Why the fuck not? What else are we gonna do? Listen to you whining all night? Hey, we're a bit like Police Academy aren't we? I'm Mahoney because I'm cool as fuck. Then we've got Tackleberry over by the window and Hooks on the couch. Not to mention Sweetchuck staring at us from the fucking doorway. Hey Benjamin Button, are you coming in to say hello or what?

We see Brittian peeping through the doorway.

Butty

Tackleberry? Tackleberry's a pussy.

John

Just stop talking about Police Academy! I'm too stressed to think straight as it is. I don't need you two shit for brains yapping on about bloody Police Academy. Am I the only one freaking out about everything that's happened?

Dave

Pretty much kid yeah!

John

We've killed people today. KILLED!

Butty

Zombies John, we've killed zombies.
I've told you already little brother,
dead is dead. Zombies are not people.
Nothing of what made them human
remains. Which means I've got no
problem drilling a crowbar into their
skulls.

John

That's cold Butty. How can you be so
heartless?

Butty

Heartless? Let me tell you a little
story. Do you remember this morning
when I saved you and George Michael
over there from those two zombies? The
man and the women?

Scene 4 - Ext - Daytime - Outside the mayonnaise factory

Flashback from episode 1 of Butty killing the female zombie with a crowbar and booting the male zombie behind the pillar.

Scene 5 - Int - Brittain's living room

Butty

I'll tell you something about that man. You see I knew him. His name was Brockers…

Scene 6 - Ext - Daytime - Lill's Café

Butty sat at a table, reading a survival manual whilst watching Brockers at another table with a mountain of newspapers.

Butty is served Spam on Toast and he peeps at Brockers from behind the survival manual.

We see Brockers frantically drawing on the pictures in the newspapers.

Butty lowers the survival manual, and a third hand pops up from behind the pages, feeding him Spam on toast before lowering again.

We get a close up of Brockers drawing dicks on anything and everything.

Butty – voice over

I used to see him at Lille's Café every morning. He'd go through the morning papers, only he wouldn't be reading them. Instead he'd draw dicks on all the pictures. He didn't discriminate either. Men, women, children, animals. If the picture had a head, then that head was getting a dick. Picture of the Queen, dick on the head, David Beckham, dick on the head, Prime Minister, dick on the head. Lottery winners, dick. Top Gear Presenters,dick after dick after dick.

Scene 7 - Int – Brittain's living room.

Butty

So when I saw Brockers this morning I knew what I had to do.

Scene 8 - Ext – Daytime – Outside the

mayonnaise factory.

We see zombie Brockers dead on the ground with Butty standing over him. Butty pulls a marker pen out of his pocket and removes the lid with his mouth, spitting it to the ground. He then leans over Brockers, drawing something on his forehead.

Shot of Butty's Face as he draws.

Shot again of Butty's hand, he pulls it away to reveal a dick on Brockers forehead.

Finishing drawing Butty stands up to reveal he has scribbled a dick on his forehead.

                    Butty

    It's what he would have wanted.

Scene 9 - Int - Brittain's living room.

                    Butty

    So there you have it. Not heartless at
                    all.

                    John

No, you're a regular Mother Teresa
aren't you. St. Butty.

Dave

Yeah, Patron Saint of zombie twatting.

Butty

I'll drink to that.

Butty pulls out his water canteen and
lifts it to his mouth, drinking from
it. John wretches at the smell coming
from it.

John

What are drinking? I can smell that
from over here it stinks like piss!

Butty

It is piss! We don't know what caused
the zombie outbreak. It could have come
from the water supply for all we know.
You're more than welcome to wet your
whistle little brother. There is an
endless supply after all.

Butty drinks from his canteen again and

breathes out as he finishes. Exhaling
with refreshment, slapping his tongue
against his teeth.

                    Butty

                    Aahhh...

                    John

        Dave, can't you smell that?

                    Dave

"I've been smoking 80 a day since I was
   12 Ace. We could be slap bang in the
middle of Lush and I wouldn't smell a
              fucking thing."

                    Butty

              Drink Dave?

                    Dave

As tempting as swigging your piss is,
   I'll pass thanks lar. Even though my
mouth is drier than a tramps flannel.

The living room door opens and Brittain
enters, rushing in to take a seat next
to John.

                    Dave

Finally decided to join us? What's your name kid?

Brittain

Brittain. Like Great Brittain but with two T's. My mum was an agoraphobic traveller who was too afraid to step outside. That's how we ended up here. She called me Brittain because she wanted me to see every inch of the UK. Unfortunately I inherited her phobia. So what's it like outside?

John

I won't lie, it's bloody horrible. Runcorn looks like a war zone

Dave

And that was before the zombie outbreak!

John

Corpses line the street, zombies are everywhere, there's people being eaten alive, building are burning, smashed up vehicles... This morning I hit a zombie across the face with a decapitated head.

Butty

Where's your mum now?

Brittain

Dead. Well undead. She's wandering
about outside somewhere. Funny really.
She's getting about more now she's dead
than she ever did when she was alive.

Dave

I have to say Ace, considered you ma'
has turned into a dead fuck you don't
seem to arsed lad.

Brittain

Well she's outside. I've always been
able to detach myself from anything
beyond my front door. Everything
outside has always been so out of
reach. Anyway, she'll be back in doors
where she belongs once the army turn up
with a vaccine to fix all of this.

John

So you've never been outside? Not once?

Brittain

Nope. Not once. I've been to places though. Well, in my mind I have. Look…

Brittain retrieves a photo album and sits on the couch next to John. He goes through the photos as described. Brittain has photoshopped himself into all the pictures.

Brittain

This is me in Egypt; Me on the Great Wall of China; that one is me with the Dalai Lama. Me with the Pope, there's one in Rio, Mount Rushmore, with JFK just before he was assassinated and this one is my favourite. It's me getting cosy with the Spice Girls.

John

Brittain, thanks again for letting us stay.

Brittain

I didn't exactly let you, you forced your way in. But I have spent a bit of time studying you from out in the hallway and I've sussed you out. You're not bad people, you just needed to be somewhere safe.

Dave

What do you mean 'sussed' us out?

Brittain

You by the window with the crazy look in your eyes and a copy of Busty Lovelies strapped to your forearm; Butty is it? I know you didn't really want to kill me but you would have done if you had to. You're the kind of person that does what needs to be done to survive and to protect your group. Emotion doesn't come in to it.

A smug Butty kept his eyes on the window throughout Brittain's appraisal nodding his head in agreement.

Brittain

You with the sunglasses on listening to that tinny music. Dave isn't it? You chain smoke and act the way you do because you think it gives you an identity. Because if you didn't then people would see the real you and you're scared that once they see how lonely and empty your life is, they

won't like you anymore and you'll lose
the small amount of friends you have.

Dave

Alright smart arse pipe down. If I
wanted to be psychoanalysed I would
have got married. And this music isn't
tinny. It's The Lexicon of Love by ABC,
one of the finest albums ever made. You
kids today wouldn't know a good song
even if Martin Fry rocked up in his
gold suit and sang it to you. It's all
One Direction these days and that Kanya
West or whatever her name is. Over
produced drivel from fame hungry no
marks. Cunts. You want to get yourself
a Walkman and a mix tape of the finest
music ever made from the greatest
decade there ever was. The fucking 80s!

Brittain

And you, John. You're the glue that
holds your little group together. Why
else would they be following you on a
suicide mission to find your daughter?

John

Suicide mission, great! Even the hermit
that's aging quicker than an Aldi
cheese thinks Emily is doomed.

                    Butty

            (Looking through the window)

          What does your mum look like?

                   Brittain

      Blonde hair, young, pretty and wearing
      a flowery dress. Last time I saw her
            she was chewing on a hand.

    Butty peeps through the curtains then
    motions for John and Dave to join him.
    They all look outside.

    Scene 10 - Ext - Early evening -
    Outside Brittain's house

    A young female zombie fitting
    Brittain's description shuffles outside
    the house, chewing on a decapitated
    hand.

    We can see John, Dave and Butty looking
    through the window.

    She turns suddenly towards the window.
    John closes the curtains quickly.

Scene 11 - Int - Brittain's living room.

John, Dave and Butty turn away from the window.

                    Dave

That's his mum? She's at least half his
                fucking age.

John, Dave and Butty look at Brittain.

Brittain looks back giving a thumbs up and a goofy grin.

                    Dave

  I need a drink. Got any booze, Europe
   or whatever your fucking name is?"

                    John

        We're in for a long night.

Fade out to black.

Scene 12 - Int - Early morning - Brittain's living room

Very loud snoring is heard.

Slow fade up from black on John's face
who is lying on the couch with his eyes
closed, he looks happy and content.
John starts to stir, opening his eyes
then looking depressed he sees where he
is. He sees Butty still sat at the
window and Dave asleep on the floor,
sat up with an unlit cigarette in his
mouth. There is a half empty bottle of
whisky by his side. Dave is the cause
of the horrendous snoring.

John

Have you been awake all night?

Butty

Well someone had to keep watch whilst
you and sleeping beauty over there
rested up.

John

You must be knackered.

Butty

I'm fine little brother. I've been
slowly weaning myself off sleep for the
last few years. I've trained myself to
sleep in small but very frequent
bursts. I've become so good at it that

I have complete control of when I go to sleep and when I wake up. I can even sleep with my eyes open. Here watch this…

Butty stares straight ahead for a few seconds.

                    Butty

See. That was five seconds kip right there. If I do it at regular intervals throughout the day, it removes the need for a full nights sleep.

                    John

Didn't you try this once before? Yeah I remember now. You were so sleep deprived you lost your marbles and was found in the cooked meats isle at Asda, naked apart from a sock puppet covering your genitals and you were singing the theme tune from The Golden Girls? You ended up barred from every Asda in the country after at.

                    Butty

Yes but I've had a lot more practice since then. Asda's shit anyway.

                    John

Suppose we best wake Dave. Dave, Dave, DAVE!

Dave jolts into life and automatically lights the cigarette in his mouth, like it was a reflex action.

                    Dave

    Morning Ace, are we off to find Emily
                    then?

                    John

      How are you not hung over after
           drinking all night?

                    Dave

    I don't get hangovers John, which is
just one of the many reasons why I'm so
            fucking awesome.

                    John

Where's Brittain anyway? I haven't seen
        him since last night?

                    Dave

    Dunno. The last thing I remember is
    trying to help him get over his

agoraphobia then I passed out
bladdered.

Scene 13 - Int - Hallway

Dave and Brittain are sat on the
stairs. Dave is bladdered, chugging on
a bottle of whisky.

Dave

Listen Kid, this agoraphobia, it's all
in your head. You sit at home watching
the news and it's all doom and gloom.
Murder, rape, robberies, terrorist
attacks… and with modern technology
there's barely any reason to leave the
house at all. More and more people work
from home these days too. I've got this
mate, Kenny his name is. Fat fella with
a bald head and a moustache. Always
sweating and he snores when he's awake.
You know the type. Anyway, he runs a
telephone sex line from his home. Big
June he calls himself. He has a voice
changer program on his computer that he
connects to his telephone line which
makes him sound like a woman. He makes
a fortune talking dirty to perverts all
day for £6.75 per minute. If only the
sticky palmed wankers knew that Big

June was actually Big Kenny and they've been stroking one out whilst he tells them the things he'd like to do to a Jaffa Cake. What I'm trying to say is you're a victim of society Kid but society doesn't exist anymore and your creature comforts are gone. What are you going to do when your food supplies run dry? Or when zombies come crashing through your windows and doors. Come on Brittain kid, wake up and smell the decay. It's time for you to make a change. There's a world outside your window and it's a world of dread and fear, but it's your world kid and it's yours for the taking!

Scene 14 - Int - Brittain's living room

Butty

He's stood outside the front door muttering to himself. He's been there for hours.

John

He's outside? Why the hell didn't you say something?

John rushes to the front door.

Scene 15 - Ext - Early morning -
Outside Brittain's house

Brittain is stood outside his house
looking up to the sky with his arms out
wide. He has a huge smile on his face.
His zombie mother is shuffling towards
him but he is so happy to be outside he
hasn't noticed.

Brittain's front door opens and John
appears. He notices the zombie
approaching.

                    John

                Brittain!

Brittain looks at John with glee.

                  Brittain

              I'm outside!

                    John

    Quickly, get your arse over here!

Brittain turns around and looks
directly at his zombie mother who is
now almost within touching distance. He
is overjoyed to see her.

                    Brittain

               Mum, I'm outside!

Brittain's mother reaches in and bites
down into his shoulder, pulling him to
the floor.

Butty, followed by Dave, runs out of
the house and removing a screwdriver
from his tool belt, rams it into
Brittain's mother's head.

Brittain lies on the floor looking up
to the sky, blood spurting from an open
wound on his shoulder.

John, Butty and Dave stand over him.

                    Brittain

             The sky, it's so pretty.

                      Dave

         Fuck me lad what were you doing
                    outside?

                    Brittain

       You told me there was a world outside
     my window and you were right, you were
                      right!

                       57

Dave

I was quoting Band Aid dick head, don't
listen to anything I say!

Butty

Two tins of spam and a copy of Filthy
GILFS says he won't make it through the
day.

Brittain coughs and sputters his last
breath before dying.

Butty

Told you. Come on, we best get moving.

John

What about him? He'll turn won't he?

Dave

I'll take care of little Jimmy Krankie.
You two crack on and I'll catch you up.

John and Butty walk away from the house
leaving Dave standing over Brittain.

Dave

Welcome to the real world Brittain lad.

Dave drills his Battle Paddle into Brittain's head.

End

Episode 3

'Once in a Lifetime'

Scene 1 - Ext - Daytime - Smart Storage yard

The shutters roll up on the entrance to Smart Storage, revealing John, Dave and Butty's feet as they wait to enter.

Scene 2 - Int - Smart Storage entrance

John Dave and Butty are at the glass doors of the entrance.

John

What are we doing here Butty? We're supposed to be looking for Emily.

Butty

And we are but first we need more supplies if we're to be successful.

Butty taps a code into the keypad and the doors open.

Butty

Wait here till I give the all clear. I won't be long.

Butty runs into Smart Storage and the doors close behind him.

Dave

Here's one good thing about the end of the world Kid, we don't have to work in the mayonnaise factory anymore. No more will you make a living eating my mayo.

John

Please don't refer to me running a quality check as eating your mayo. The job was bad enough without having to imagine I was swallowing your junk. You know how much I hate mayonnaise. It looks like walrus jizz and tastes like tippex.

Dave

How you know what walrus jizz looks like I don't know but I can assure you my jizz looks nothing like that. It looks more like wall paper paste and tastes like, well… fuck knows. Benson & Hedges probably.

John

Why are we talking about your jizz?

Dave

Hey you brought it into the equation Ace, I was talking about you not having to eat mayonnaise for a living. I never did understand why you worked at the factory, it was obvious you fucking hated it. Despite appearances you're not a complete dip shit.

John

You worked there too remember.

Dave

That's right, I, along with my trusted battle paddle here, made all the mayo. I liked it kid. Hours were good, money was decent and the work was a piece of piss. Plus I got to talk bollocks all day. What more could I ask for?

John

Well you do love to talk bollocks. You should talk to my brother, he chats just as much shit as you.

Dave

I would if I could catch him. He's
having too much fun twatting dead
fucks.

Scene 3 - Int - Smart Storage

A zombie shuffles along a corridor and
turns a corner. Butty is creeping
behind the zombie, slowly and quietly
catching it up.

Now right behind the zombie, Butty
takes out his crowbar and inserts it
into the back of the zombie's head. The
zombie drops to the floor, dead.

Scene 4 - Int - Smart Storage entrance

Dave

Don't tell him I said this but I'm
starting to like your brother. Sure
he's nuttier than a Walnut Whip but
he's pretty handy at killing zombies
where as you… well… you're like the
Frank Spencer of the apocalypse.

John

We can't all come to terms with the end of the world as quickly as you two have. This morning I was just a single father from Runcorn, working a shit job to support his daughter. Now I'm an endangered species! Zombies Dave! This can't be happening. Are you sure it's not something else?

Scene 5 – Int – Smart Storage

Butty is hiding behind a corner as a zombie approaches. As the zombie reaches Butty's location, he sticks his porno mag covered arm out into the zombie's mouth. Whilst the zombie gnaws on top shelf armour, Butty knifes him in the head. The dead zombie falls to the floor.

Scene 6 – Int – Smart Storage entrance

Dave

Oh it's zombies alright, it's a classic case.

                    John

      Classic case? You make it sound like
          this happens all the time!

                    Dave

      The world has been preparing us for
      this shit for years John. Movies, video
      games, TV shows… the list goes on Ace.
       The fucking Walking Dead is on the
       telly every week and you think this
       could be something else? I hope your
      daughter is more clued up than you are
       kid. Where are we headed anyway?

                    John

      She left for college yesterday morning,
      said she had hockey practice. If we're
       going to find her the best thing to do
      is try and retrace her steps. Once my
          brother stops pissing about.

Scene 7 - Int - Smart Storage

A zombie shuffles along a corridor
before being joined by another zombie;
something has their attention.

A wide shot reveals a dead body on the ground. Both zombies move in, kneeling down and ripping into the body's stomach, shovelling innards and intestines into their mouths.

Butty turns a corner and see's the 2 hungry zombies. Brandishing a baseball bat he runs at them, taking them out one at a time with 2 clean strikes to the head.

Scene 8 - Int - Smart Storage entrance

                    John

    What the hell is he doing? We don't
           have time for this!

Butty appears at the glass doors and inputs the code to open them.

                   Butty

     The coast is clear. Let's move.

John and Dave follow him inside.

Scene 9 - Int - Smart Storage

The gang walk a corridor. There is a dead body lay face down on a trolley. As they walk passed the body it comes to life, reaching out to grab their legs.

Butty places a foot on the zombie's neck and drills his crowbar into the back of its head.

Butty

Now firstly, we need to keep the noise down. This is a big old building and sound travels. If there are any more zombies in here the last thing we want to do is alert them to our whereabouts. Now then, have I got something to show you.

Butty walks forward leaving John and Dave stood at the entrance to the corridor. Dave makes a gesture that suggests Butty has a small penis and both he and John laugh before following him.

They turn a corner and enter a corridor with many storage units on both sides.

                    Butty

  Welcome to Butty's lair! Along this
  corridor you will find storage units
  containing supplies for every end of
  the world scenario you can think of.

Butty walks the corridor pointing at
the storage units whilst going through
the list below.

John and Dave look at each. John thinks
his brother has completely flipped and
Dave is loving it. They follow Butty.

                    Butty

Robot uprising, alien invasion, nuclear
war, vampires, werewolves, demon ginger
  kids, spider badgers, mutated women
with laser tits, flesh eating penguins,
   radioactive Yorkshire men, lizard
bastards... and this is what we're here
for. My zombie apocalypse survival lock
                     up.

Butty opens the lock up and we see
inside, revealing a room full of large
boxes labelled...

Crowbars small

Crowbars medium

Crowbars large

Porno Mags

Piss

And the majority of boxes are labelled 'SPAM'.

Dave

That sure is a lot of spam ace! There's more pork in there than Scotland Yard!"

Butty

You'll be grateful for all that spam in a few months when food supplies are depleted. Up to five years those tins of delicious salty pork goodness can last. Five years! They have a longer life expectancy than most of the human race.

John

I can't live on Spam for the rest of my days. I mean it's nice and everything but the same thing day after day… I'll end up hating it more than I hate mayonnaise.

Butty

I'll have you know that Spam is extremely versatile. You can use it to make omelettes, enchiladas, burgers and even a curry.

Dave

Spam curry? Fuck Off! My hoop is pulsing like a cartoon thumb just thinking about it!

Butty

Come on, grab as many supplies as you can. There's a holdall in here somewhere. Oh, and here, have one of these…

Butty reaches into the lock up and produces 2 children's walky talkys, handing them to John and Dave.

Butty

In case we get separated.

John

Separated? Dave's got a 1986 Motorola the size of a house brick. That's got a better range than these.

Dave

Amen Kidda

Butty

They work just fine little brother.
I've replaced the antennas, wired them
to a higher voltage power supply and
generally pepped them up a bit. Come
on, let's get a move on.

Dave looks into the lock up and sees a
dildo. He grabs it and starts wobbling
it about.

Dave

Weyhey what the fuck is this for lar!
Are you gonna use it fuck a zombie's
brains out?

Butty snatches it from Dave and points
it at him, jiggling it about.

Butty

Pretty much. Weaponry, comes in many
forms, shapes and sizes. We must make
use of everything we have at our
disposal.

Dave snatches it back.

                    Dave

          Whatever dick head!

Dave licks the sucky pad of the dildo
then sticks it to Butty's helmet. John
and Dave laugh really load. Butty
doesn't react.

Loud groans echoe through the corridor.
John and Dave look at each other with
concern.

                   Butty

     I bloody told you to be quiet!

Groaning is heard again. Butty closes
the lock up and walks to the end of the
corridor, looking around a corner. We
see 2 zombies heading his way.

                   Butty

   Run! Find an empty lock up and hide,
  I'll come and find you. Reach me on the
                 walky talky.

Butty pulls out 2 sawn off snooker cues
from behind his back and runs at the
zombies.

Scene 11 - Int - Smart Storage

John and Dave turn around and run along the corridor, turning left out of sight. Moments later they run right followed by three zombies. (Scooby do style).

John and Dave run into an empty corridor and catch their breath.

                    John

I think we've lost them. Where the hell
                 are we?

                    Dave

Not a fucking clue. Everywhere looks
the same in here. Like a Manchester
            council estate!

1 zombie appears at the far end of the corridor, shuffling towards them. They turn around to see another 2 zombies at the other end of the corridor, moving closer.

                    Dave

              Fuck my hat!

                    John

What are going to do?

                    Dave

    Cack our pants judging by the smell
    you're letting off. What was it Sir
            Spam-A-Lot said?

Dave and John pull on lock up doors as
the zombies move closer and closer. At
the last minute they find one that is
open, rushing inside and closing the
door.

Scene 12 - Int - Lock up

Dave shuts the door and both he and
John put their backs against it, adding
extra pressure to keep the zombies out.
Lights are low and zombies pound
against the door.

                    John

        Great, now we're trapped

                    Dave

    They'll get bored soon enough and fuck
                    off.

John

I'm not sure zombies get bored Dave.
There must be something in here we can
use to defend ourselves?

Dave pulls out his walky talky. John
searches the lock up.

Dave

(Into the walky talky)

Dave to crazy Ace, come in Crazy Ace?
Butty do you read me… ah it's not
fucking working! Batteries must be flat
kid. Where's yours?

John

I think I dropped it outside.

Dave

"If we're gonna fight our way out then
the Battle Paddle is good lar but I
doubt I could defend us both, not
against three dead fucks, not at once."

John looks over several large boxes.

John

You won't need to, I've had an idea.

A-Team-esq montage.

Close up of John pulling rolls of cello tape, biting through it, wiping sweat from his brow, close ups of his face concentrating on the task at hand. We can hear the ripping of material and the tearing of cello tape over the noise of zombies outside, occasionally cutting to Dave's face looking impressed at John's creation.

Montage ends.

Dave nods at John approvingly.

                    Dave

  Not bad kidda not bad. Right, let's do
   this Johnny boy. It's zombie twatting
                    time!

Scene 13 - Int - Lock up / corridor - Smart Storage

Dave pulls the lock up door open to reveal Butty standing victorious over a pile of dead zombies. He is holding a blood dripping dildo.

We get a shot from Butty's point of view of Dave and John stood in the lock up doorway. Dave is wielding his paddle and John is covered in bubble wrap, only his head is exposed.

                    Butty

Very good little brother, I like your thinking but you're wrapped up a little too tight around the leg area. Zombies will have ripped through that bubble wrap before you've taken a few steps. Use your head John and always ask yourself, what would Butty do? We still need to tool up, come with me.

Butty tosses John his walky talky that was dropped earlier then walks away.

                    Dave

          After you, Stay Puft.

Dave motions for John to go first and follow Butty.

Dave pauses and looks at the pile of zombies. Bending down to search through their clothes he finds a packet of cigarettes.

Dave

You fucking beauty!

He kisses the packet of cigarettes and walks away.

Scene 14 - Ext - Smart storage yard

The shutter rolls up and we see the gangs feet, ready to leave the lock up.

Shot from behind the gang, we see the roller slowly rising to reveal the yard is filled with zombies, but they all have their backs to John, Dave and Butty. Something has their attention.

Dave presses the button that operates the shutters and they lower again.

John

This doesn't look good. We need to turn back, we can't take on that many.

Dave

By 'we' you mean me and Butty. The only
thing you've killed lately is my buzz
with your constant fucking whining. And
turn back where? Inside? There's
nothing in their but dead fucks and
boxes of your brother's piss!

Butty presses the button and the
shutters raise again.

John

What are you doing?

The shutters rise and we see the horde
of zombies again.

The hungry horde turn to look at John,
Dave and Butty. Our heroes look at each
other, brandish their weapons then run
at the horde.

Freeze frame on John, Dave and Butty as
they are about to do battle.

Text on screen reads

To be continued?

End.

Lightning Source UK Ltd.
Milton Keynes UK
UKHW03f1853140318
319465UK00001B/68/P